LOVE, HATE,
AND APATHY

LOVE, HATE, AND APATHY

S. Hale Humphrey-Jones

Love, Hate, and Apathy

Copyright © 2024 by S. Hale Humphrey-Jones. All rights reserved.

No part of this publication may be reproduced, stored in a retrieval system or transmitted in any way by any means, electronic, mechanical, photocopy, recording or otherwise without the prior permission of the author except as provided by USA copyright law.

The opinions expressed by the author are not necessarily those of URLink Print and Media.

1603 Capitol Ave., Suite 310 Cheyenne, Wyoming USA 82001
1-888-980-6523 | admin@urlinkpublishing.com

URLink Print and Media is committed to excellence in the publishing industry.

Book design copyright © 2024 by URLink Print and Media. All rights reserved.

Published in the United States of America

Library of Congress Control Number: 2024903493
ISBN 978-1-68486-698-4 (Paperback)
ISBN 978-1-68486-703-5 (Digital)

05.12.23

PROLOGUE

No woman willingly enters into an abusive relationship. There are no clanging alarm bells or flashing lights. The abuse doesn't magically materialize at the first smile or the first touch of her hand. Rather, it emerges as the slow and insidious reptile that it is to become, slithering into its deadly coil until without warning—IT STRIKES.

There are at first deep declarations of love, a suggestion that it is the two of you against a world of neglect and misunderstanding. *Only I can truly know and love you as you are.* Gradually, her world of friends and family are perceived as a threat to their perfect and universally intended love. *They are trying to come between us. They don't understand that we are meant to be; we are soul mates.*

Attention, no matter how innocent, from the opposite sex brings intense anger and jealousy. Sometimes, what is perceived as even a minor flirtation, a compliment or a smile, can evoke the first act of violence. It may be a slap, a shove, or an outburst of rage resulting in a broken object. Or, it may be as subtle as a sullen withdrawal of affection.

Often the blame is turned on her. *You made me do it. I can't bear to see you with someone else. I couldn't live if you left me.*

The abuse may not always be physical or overtly aggressive. The strength is in the power of control over her actions and emotions. A small rebuke or ridicule. *That outfit makes you look fat or slutty. I didn't realize how little you know. It is cute. That's why you need me. Its ok. I love you anyway. No one else will love you in spite of it.*

Her self-esteem, confidence, and, most importantly, social support system becomes eroded. Until, there is nothing left but the desire to please him, and the constant worry that he will be displeased by what she does. She begins to monitor herself, her time, her friends, her wardrobe.

Why doesn't she leave? Where will she go? Who will want her? How could she survive without him? Most importantly, what if he kills me? What may have started out as love, may have become hate.

Sometimes there is an absence of all emotion, a feeling void of all caring, an emptiness. There is no love or hate. The opposite of love, however, is not hate. It is apathy.

CATHERINE

I don't belong here. This was a mistake. I paced the cold, damp room in the basement of an old church. I don't know why I let Carol talk me into this meeting. The chill caused me to button my coat, shivering. The walls were a dull beige color that once was something nearing a cream shade of white, the paint peeling in spots. The whole atmosphere was very unappealing.

The folding chairs were all arranged in a circle. At one end of the room a long table held a belching coffee pot surrounded by paper cups and assorted accessories. The coffee actually smelled good, but wasn't strong enough to overcome the musty scent.

The room was empty, but someone had been here recently to set up the chairs and coffee. I headed for the door. I could get out before anyone saw me and just tell Carol it wasn't for me after all. Too late, the door swung open and the sound of voices pushed me back toward one of the folding chairs. I would have to get through this one meeting after all.

I watched, mesmerized, as each of the women told her story. Looking at these brave women I could see they wore their bruises and scars as banners of their devastating battle. Some were fresh, dark and red. Others fading and healing into a yellow reminder. Most with long sleeves to hide their visible shame.

One young woman, Susan, potentially pretty, but with ashen skin and lank brown hair, brandished a new cast on her right wrist. She had that vacant stare of a woman who has given up. Her clothes were clean but un-ironed and clearly several sizes too large. The gaunt look indicated that she had lost a lot of weight. Probably unintentional.

Another, Mazy, a flaming redhead, repeatedly rubbed a deep, white scar which ran down the left side of her neck. Her eyes, which may have once been a bright blue, were watery and shot with red.

The stories differed in many ways, yet were hauntingly similar in others. They all agreed, however, that in the beginning it was beautiful, and they were deeply and uncontrollably in love.

That was certainly the case with Bob. So much in love. How could something so wonderful, so beautiful erode into such a nightmare? Unlike the others, though, my wounds weren't physical; mine were all inside, like a raging infection that terrorized me at night and stalked me throughout my long exhausting days.

It was now my turn. I looked around at the group of women in the circle. The strong odor of coffee, was now mixed with the intense smell of fear.

I could feel the group turning toward me as Janice, the facilitator, asked what brought me to the group. The heat in my face flamed. God, why did I have to blush so easily. I'd always hated the fairness of my skin, which never seemed to match my dark curly hair. No wonder Bob got so unhappy with me.

"Would you like to share with the group, Catherine?"

"I don't think I belong here," I stammered, the blush creating a sheen of moisture which trickled down my back and neck. "Bob never hurt me like that. He never hit me. Never."

"Yet on the phone you said you were afraid of him."

"Yes, since we divorced, he seems to be everywhere, just staring at me. He doesn't say anything and he doesn't come near me. He just looks. Not smiling, not even frowning. Just looks. Sometimes, I don't even see him, but I just know he is there. I feel him."

"And the phone calls?"

"I don't even know they're from him. They could be kids, crank calls. When I tried to report it, the police said they couldn't even issue a restraining order since he hasn't actually done anything. No actual threats or anything. I don't know why I am so afraid; he never hurt me, not like that." I could feel the tears dripping down my flushed face. So embarrassing! Why did I even come here?

"How has he hurt you, Catherine? You keep saying he hasn't hurt you like *that*. How has he hurt you?"

I looked up, astonished. How could she know?

"Well, at first it was just little things. He always wanted to know where I was; he seemed to think I was lying to him. I felt so bad that I'd upset him, so I tried to be on time and to let him know where I was. Then it was what I wore. He'd always loved my clothes, the bright colors, the soft fabrics. He said they brought out my blue eyes. Then he kept saying I was dressing to attract other men. I was so confused."

The tears were now sobs that I couldn't seem to control. Why do I have to be such a baby?

"Then, when I tried to wear more subtle clothes, he said I was dull and boring. I tried to be what he wanted; I just didn't know how. Nothing seemed to please him. Nothing. What did I do wrong?"

The other women were nodding now. They seemed to understand even though I was more confused than ever. Mazy, the redhead was scowling. She kept banging her fist on the arm of the chair.

"I think we've all felt the same confusion," Janice added, passing me a tissue. I smiled my thanks. She had a very soothing manner, and an air of confidence that was both comforting and supportive. She had soft brown hair, and looked to be in her early fifties. Something of a mother figure. You felt you could trust her, and even maybe depend on her.

When I merely nodded in agreement, she straightened up.

"OK, I think we need to wrap it up for now. Same time next week? Stay safe all of you. Catherine, you are exactly where you need to be."

They walked together into the night, each guarding the other while they found their individual modes of transportation. Those who drove started their cars but waited until all lights were on as they moved out in unison. Others stood at the bus stop but no woman was left alone. Catherine was grateful for their support as she got in her car and drove to her small apartment.

BOB

Hatred! The bitterness tormented Bob's very being. It haunted his dreams in fitful spurts throughout the night. The hatred occupied his awareness with the first yawn of each new day. During his waking hours, the hatred bubbled forth in a white, foul smelling, sticky substance that seemed to find its permanent place in the corner of his mouth. He often caught himself reaching to wipe away the goop at regular intervals, only to find it reappeared moments later.

Catherine was gone. He'd wanted her gone, but not this way. He wanted her gone in his way. He wanted her to suffer. He craved revenge stronger than he'd craved cigarettes, a longing that never really disappeared.

She'd just walked away, in that damned annoying manner she had. A carriage that announced clearly, without question, that she was better than him. Oh, Catherine had always denied feeling superior, but he suspected she knew deep down that she was. How he despised her for that.

As much as Bob loved Catherine, and God how he loved her, he hated her more. The line between love and hate was getting thinner all the time. Mostly, he wanted her to suffer. He would leave her with nothing. That would fix her good.

Damn her, though, she didn't seem to care that he'd tricked her into leaving before the twenty years were up, before he would be forced to pay alimony. She said she hadn't wanted money from him, didn't want anything but freedom. She sure made that clear enough. Yes, she wanted to be free of him.

Why hadn't she begged, the way he'd dreamed? Begged him to take her back, not to abandon her. Told him how much she loved him and needed him. For that, he despised her.

. He recalled the times he'd made her cry. Catherine's anguished tears flowed through his memory. What a beautiful sight. What power. Just the thought of her crumpled, tear stained, face made him hum with joy

There was that one night; it was glorious. They'd been in her favorite restaurant, and he made one stupid mistake while ordering, pronounced something incorrectly. The waiter corrected him. Catherine hadn't said a word, but he caught that familiar look, just a little up and to the side. A soft sigh of resignation was the only sound that passed her lips. Did she think he was a moron? Why did she insist on making him feel so ignorant? Nothing made him more furious than being made to feel stupid.

Pulling out all the stops, he began his retaliation. "Why do you keep taking those worthless classes. You know you'll never make any money. Nobody in the real world gives a damn about those useless poets"

He'd continued in this vein until, spotting that tiny quiver on her lower lip, he upped the ante and began raising his voice.

Catherine had looked around, humiliated. A scene in a restaurant, or any public place, was the one thing that would upset her. Now, he could tell she was fighting the tears. Her jaw tightened. Then she pressed her lips together and began to twist her napkin.

Looking up at him with that pleading look she whispered. "Please. Don't do this. Not here. Not now."

A tiny tear escaped one bright blue eye. She twirled her raven curls, tugging them behind one ear. She'd always done that when she was upset. He knew, then, that he'd won. He had the power.

He'd kept it up until they were home where her tears fully erupted. She slept in the guestroom again that night. That night, that was worth it. That night, he won.

Yes, Bob had always felt superior when Catherine cried. But this quiet calm made him feel small. Almost as much as the anger, he'd felt confusion. He'd always known that Catherine was using him. She married him for his money, no doubt about that. Well, he didn't really have any money when they married, but he managed to ignore that fact. He knew she'd been using him all along. No matter how often she denied it, he knew she'd cheated on him. The rage grew when he thought about the love note.

Borrowing her key so he could warm her car for her before going to work, he returned to find she was in the shower. Not wanting to disturb her, Bob intended to stick the key in one of the zipper compartments of her purse. The blue paper was stuck in the zipper. Catherine never used colored paper. She thought it was cheap. Freeing the document from the zipper, he read the note, still clutching her key.

> *Can't wait until I see you again*, the note began. *Hearing you speak captivates me. You are so poetic. I will love you, always.* There was no signature.

Bob had waited for her, note in hand when she came out of the shower. The look of surprise on Catherine's face angered him even more. Why wouldn't she just be honest?

"I have never seen that note before. Someone must have stuck it in my purse. I never even use that zipper compartment. The thing always sticks."

Bob knew she was lying. Craving confirmation of her betrayal, he began to follow her.

CATHERINE

As I closed the door behind me, I realized I had been clutching my keys so tightly they left marks in my palm. Letting out my breath in a whoosh, I sank into the nearest chair. Safe, for now. He wasn't outside, at least not that I could see, but, somehow, I could feel him near me. It was as though he was touching me with his mind. It wasn't a loving touch.

When had it all changed? We were so in love once. How long ago? What did I do wrong to make him turn so vehemently?

So exhausted, I was even too tired to walk to the bedroom. Kicking off my shoes I grabbed my cushion and flopped down on the sofa, clothes and all. As usual, sleep hovered just out of my reach as his face appeared before me. Memories.

The first time I saw him he was walking across the lawn of my parent's home. I guessed he was one of the contractors who had bid on my father's new gazebo. I couldn't exactly call him handsome, and he was nothing like the men I had dated. Hah. Maybe that was the original attraction. He was different. Not too tall, but stocky, muscular, with dark hair that desperately needed a trim, and a growth that was several days without a shave.

But he was magnificent! His gait, his fierce look, those flashing black eyes. Wow! I could feel my heart actually shaking.

I barely remember standing. My legs were so weak I thought I might fall back into the lawn chair. We gazed at each other for moments, transported to another time and place, as though we weren't really there. Then he reached out his hand and immediately withdrew it in embarrassment. It was covered in grime.

I didn't care about the dirt on his hands. They looked beautiful to me, all calloused and strong. Not like the manicured smooth hands of the bankers and accountants my father brought home. I just shook my head and took his hand, holding it until my mother came and called me inside. I hadn't even heard his voice.

Bob never got the job, but, somehow, he found me again. He was waiting in his truck when I walked outside. I just climbed in without a word and we drove away. I don't remember how long we drove, but he stopped in front of a small stream surrounded by trees and wild flowers. I could see that he had showered and shaved. His hair was still too long and somewhat unruly, but his jaw was strong, the calloused hands well-scrubbed.

When I heard his voice for the first time, any resistance that I might have had was obliterated. It was a warm, soft growl that reached deep into my being. Then he touched me. Those hard, calloused hands were so gentle and yet so confident. I was in his arms in an instant. I was his.

After that we were inseparable. My father was in a rage. He threatened to destroy Bob. He threatened to disinherit me. We didn't care about any of it. We were married before the end of summer. My parents were not there, and I was told that my last year of college would not be covered. I was on my own.

BOB

Bob couldn't believe his fortune. He'd never dreamed he could have a woman like Catherine. So beautiful, so cultured, so smart. She loved HIM, no one else. He just had to be sure it would always be like that. She was HIS.

In the first year it was idyllic. She looked at him as though he were a god or something. When he told Cathy he would pay for her to finish school, the tears in her eyes made it worth all the tuition and time it took away from him. He was her hero.

But then he began to worry. He knew exactly how long it took to get from campus to home and began to call to be sure she was safe. What took her so long? Was she talking to someone? Bob knew there were young educated guys all over the campus. Maybe he shouldn't have encouraged her to go back to school. Would she find someone else, someone better? Would she leave him? He had to make her safe. She had to be his, and only his.

Catherine kept making references to writers and poets and quoting from some stupid book she was reading. The frustration began to tighten in his stomach like a vise. Popping Tums regularly, Bob tried to control his growing anger against this unknown enemy. Sarcasm erupted more and more frequently. "What do they know about the real world? Maybe you should take some courses in something worthwhile."

He knew it would be ok when she graduated. She would come back to him then. He only had to wait. But when Bob discovered

Catherine had been offered a job as an adjunct teacher, with the condition that she went to graduate school, he couldn't control his rage.

"No, no, no. Absolutely not. I will not pay another cent to that snobbish school. They are just trying to turn you against me. No!"

Catherine only smiled and told him he would no longer need to pay tuition. The college where she would begin working would pay for her continued education as long as she worked there.

"My wife doesn't need to work. Don't you think I can take care of you?

She wanted to work, she insisted. That's when Bob began to suspect. She must be seeing someone, someone who can quote poetry to her. She didn't respect him anymore. He was no longer her hero.

CATHERINE

I couldn't believe Bob's reaction when I told him about graduate school. The increasing sarcasm about my classes sparked a new sense of tension and anxiety. Bob had changed. Was it my fault? Maybe I needed to show him more affection. I tried dressing up for him, but that triggered a rage that I had never experienced before from anyone. For the first time since our marriage, I began to fear him.

He became so unpredictable. We would be having dinner out as a kind of date night. It would start out loving and fun, but then something would change. I could feel a charge in the air, like before an electrical storm. I knew it was coming.

Trying not to anger him, I searched for neutral subjects, small talk. I complemented him on his new haircut, his shirt. The more I tried the louder he became. I would cringe waiting for the next onslaught which I feared would go on for hours after we left the restaurant. The food in my stomach turned to an acid ball and I could no longer eat.

Then he would growl that he paid for a meal that I didn't even appreciate. It wasn't good enough, he wasn't good enough, and so on.

Bob seemed to constantly need reassurance, and I tried. His business had become very successful and I told him over and over how proud I was of his acumen. But then he would sneer and talk about how the Ivory Tower people I worked with would never make any money.

I felt like such a failure. What was I doing wrong? What had happened to the warm, loving man I married? What could I do?

I felt so alone. I needed someone to talk to. After two years of silence, I called my mother. I needed to hear her voice, needed some comfort and guidance. I loved my mother and I knew she loved me, but I also knew how much she feared my father's wrath.

I knew she wouldn't recognize my number, and I hoped she would answer. Even if she didn't want to talk to me, perhaps she would at least listen since I knew my father wouldn't be at home at this hour. The phone rang several times, and I guessed she was out, but then she picked up. Her voice sounded breathless, as though she'd been running. "Yes."

"Mama. Its me, Catherine."

"Cathy, baby, are you all right?"

"Yes Mama, I'm fine. I just wanted to talk."

"Are you still with that man?"

"Yes, Mama, just talk to me, please."

"Catherine, my precious girl, I love you so much, but unless you've come to your senses, I can't. I'm sorry." The line went dead.

"Mama, Mama please." I hung up the phone and sobbed for an hour before I realized I was alone in this. I just knew it was going to get worse, and I had no idea how to stop it.

It became more and more difficult to study at home as Bob felt I was neglecting him. I began to spend more time at the school library or faculty lounge. In the lounge everyone sat with a book in front of them or processing an idea out loud. We all laughed and joked. We shared opinions, debated, and agreed. It became my refuge. Home had become my hell.

Then, there was the note. Occasionally, it became apparent that a student would develop a crush on one of the instructors. Usually it was innocent, and there was nothing overt and would end when the specific class was completed. Once, however, someone wrote a note, something of a love note, and stuck it in my purse.

I would often leave my purse laying around as it never occurred to me that anyone would take it. I didn't carry much cash or anything of any real value. The funny thing was that I had no idea it was there until Bob discovered it. The note had been stuck in a zipper compartment that I seldom used as the zipper stuck, so it could have been in there for a while. It wasn't signed and I didn't recognize the writing.

Bob was waiting for me as I began to leave for school. He was shaking the note at me, his face red with fury.

"You lied to me. You fucking cunt. You are cheating on me. Me. I have given you everything. I put you through your last year of school. You wouldn't even have this stupid job if it weren't for me. This is how you thank me? This? He shoved the note in my face.

I took the note from him, mutely staring. "Bobby, honey, I have never seen this before."

"You lying Bitch!"

I was sure he would hit me then and began to sob. But then he turned and stomped out of the house.

I ran to the bathroom and emptied my breakfast and sat on the toilet gasping for breath. What am I going to do? I was not late for work, but I had to get out of the house. So, I splashed water on my face, rinsed my mouth and left the house. Each time I walked outside I breathed a sigh of relief. I was free.

THE GROUP

The group was unusually quiet tonight. There was no chatter and as the facilitator, Janice, entered she could sense the tension. A petite, dark haired woman, she somehow emanated a power defying her size. Tonight, Janice was grim. She knew the reason the others were quiet. One of their members was absent. She wouldn't be returning.

Taking a deep breath, Janice addressed the fear radiating throughout the room.

"You all must have heard about Alicia," Janice began. "In case you are not all aware of the details, let me tell you what happened. As you know Alicia was planning her escape. She had worked it out carefully. After the restraining order, he had put her in the hospital. So, she knew she needed to run before they let him out of jail."

They were all shaking their heads, and rubbing the chill from their hands. This was their biggest fear.

"He made bail and got out sooner than she expected. He caught her just as she was taking her suitcase out to the car. He dragged her inside and pulled his gun out of the hiding place in the closet. Before he shot her, he wanted to be sure she suffered. He broke her other arm and battered the rest of her face." Janice looked around the room.

"I know how hard it is to hear these horrible details, but you need to know how important a safe plan is to your survival."

"She did plan," Rosemary murmured. "What good did it do her?" Rosemary was one of the ones who continued to live with her abuser. Terrified to leave. A frail, nervous, dishwater blonde, she appeared to be a decade older than her 26 years. She stared at the facilitator, looking for answers.

Janice sighed in agreement. "Yes, she had a plan, and she might have made it, if he'd been five minutes later. If they had warned her that he'd made bail. If…. There is always a risk. We need to learn from Alicia. Let's discuss how it might have worked. We need to take back our power. But it won't be easy. We all know that."

Rosemary shook her head. "No, there is no way. He will never let me go. He still thinks I am going to a book club every week. If he finds out where I am, he will kill me, too." She stood up. I can't be here, I can't." She began to cry as the group surrounded her and encouraged her to stay.

"I know some of you are still living with your abuser. This group is risky for you, I understand that. You are on a group text. If you text 911, we will get help to you. We will locate you from your phone. We will help you."

"Alicia never had the chance to text. He got to her too fast."

The group mumbled their agreement and the fear was palpable in the room. Janice knew some of them would not return. Her hope was to save the ones she could, and she knew it wouldn't be easy. Just coming to these meetings was a huge risk. They could be followed. We could all be in jeopardy. But this was all most of them had. Their only connection to safety and freedom. Most of their friends and families had given up on them, blamed them for not leaving sooner. She needed to keep them in the group as long as she could.

CATHERINE

I couldn't believe what I'd just heard. Poor Alicia, murdered by her own husband. How can that be? I barely knew her, but she seemed so brave and hopeful at the last meeting. I felt so cold and I was shaking so hard I bit my lip. I can't go back to that group. Bob would never hurt me, though. He wouldn't. Would he?

Bob never hit me, except that one time. But it was my fault and I never told anyone.

We were in Chicago at a builders' conference Bob wanted to attend. We had just finished dinner and were walking down the street. We came to a busy intersection. There were cars coming from both directions, but Bob insisted that we run across. I resisted and he kept pulling my arm and pushing me toward the street. I panicked, screamed at him and pinched the arm he held me with.

The next thing I knew I was spinning across the street. Cars were braking and people were staring. Bob had yelled at me when I pinched him and punched the back of my head with his fist. I was so shocked I almost skidded to the curb, but then I saw the horrified faces of the people around me and I righted myself and quickly assured them I was ok.

Bob was furious, and told everyone to back off, that I was fine. He grabbed my hand and hailed a taxi. We sped away from the scene. Neither of us spoke until we were in our hotel room.

"You brought this on yourself, Cathy. You can't pinch me like that."

I was crying hard by then. "I know, Bobby, I know. I was just so scared. It was my fault. I know that. I'm sorry."

This seemed to appease him and he began pulling me toward the bed. Sex was the one way he let me make it up to him when I'd done something he hated.

Usually, sex was great with us. He was always the sexiest man I'd ever known. When he looked at me with those dark eyes, I melted. When he wanted sex, those eyes seemed to actually darken and become even blacker. That was when it was good.

When he wanted to punish me, and to prove his power over me, those dark eyes could take on a menacing look and seem to harden, like angry coals. This was his look tonight. I had no desire to have sex with him this night, but knew that to resist would be futile. After sex, he always seemed relieved, as though he'd proven his ownership of me. I hated that.

I had convinced myself that this one act of violence was an aberration, but now I wondered. There had been other times when I was certain he would hit me, but he seemed to find other ways to control me—until he didn't.

THE GROUP

Janice began the group by asking how many had actually managed to leave. Several raised their hands, others looked embarrassed and shook their heads.

"Okay, I know leaving is the hardest thing any of you can or could do. Let's share how you managed to get out. Susan, I see you've had your cast removed, and you raised your hand. How did you get out?"

"I was actually one of the lucky ones. When I went into the emergency room, someone contacted the police. He is now in jail and without bail.

I am moving out of the house before he gets out. I changed jobs, phone numbers, and I'm living with my brother. Since the emergency room had a record of the other incidents where he hurt me, he is considered a repeat offender. I'm praying he will be given a long sentence, but know I might not be notified if he is released so I am not wasting time. I don't want to end up like Alicia. I know next time he will kill me."

The group looked at Susan with a combination of admiration and envy. Susan no longer looked old and haggard. She'd had her hair done and was wearing new clothes. She smiled a lot. It was good to see.

Then Mazy began to speak slowly and quietly. Mazy was older than the others in the group; her red hair, shot through with gun metal gray, hung in dry strands about her worn face. "I tried leaving once. I moved out and changed jobs. He found out where I was working and was waiting in my car." She rubbed the long scar on her neck. "That's when I got this. He picks me up from work now. The only way I get to come here is when he is at work. My sister picks me up and gets me home before him. I am planning my next escape. Soon."

"Thank you, Mazy. This is not an easy decision. It is important to have a solid safety plan in place. Most of you are at risk of your safety and lives and have realized that leaving is your only means of survival.

My next question may surprise you, but I need to ask. How many of you are still in love with your abuser?"

Rosemary hung her head down and mumbled something. Then she looked up, tears blurring her bloodshot eyes. "God help me, I know I should hate him for what he's done to me, but I love him still. I know he loves me." She shook her head at the outraged comments of some of the others. "Yes, I know, I know, but I do believe he loves me, and when he hurts me, sometimes he's really nice, and I think maybe it will be all right. He may end up killing me someday, but I can't leave him, I can't." She sobbed loudly now, and the group looked sad for her.

"It is a fine line between love and hate, and it is often hard to accept that someone can care about you an still inflict such harm. I can't judge you, Rosemary. You have to make that decision yourself, but promise me you will keep coming here."

Rosemary shook her head in agreement.

"Catherine, you are the only one that does not acknowledge physical abuse, what was the incentive for your escape?"

"I'm not really sure how to answer that question; I never really thought of it as an escape. Can I think about that?" The group all nodded their assent as they all knew how conflicting the feelings were, and how hard it was to acknowledge that they were really the victims of abuse.

CATHERINE

I left the group trying desperately to formulate an answer to Janice's question. For most of the past ten years of our marriage I had desperately tried to fix whatever problem I had caused between Bob and me. I knew I had done something wrong; it had to be my fault. I kept remembering how wonderful he had been in the beginning. My thoughts began to change when I finished my master's.

I so desperately wanted to go to the graduation. Bob had been sick when I received my undergraduate degree and I didn't feel it fair to leave him. This time, though he made it clear that I was not to attend the ceremony.

"It is just one more humiliation. Just another method of putting me down. Reminding me that I am so uneducated. Remember, though, I am the one that built this house, and bought the clothes you wear, and pay for the fancy dinners out."

He went on for over an hour before I gave in. I sobbed the morning I would have received my degree. I sobbed again when it arrived in the mail.

The following week, I sat in the faculty lounge with a few members who were teaching summer courses. Several asked where I had been during graduation.

Carol a tall attractive blonde, taught psychology at the same school. We hung out a lot in the lounge, and tried to eat lunch together whenever possible. She always acted uncomfortable when I talked about Bob. I knew she didn't approve of him. She seemed to worry about me. It was nice to have a friend. She was the first to ask where I had been during graduation.

"I kept waiting to see you, but you weren't there."

"Bob didn't want me to go, so I stayed home."

I couldn't avoid the pity in their eyes. Carol, though looked more angry than pitying.

"That's it. Catherine, you need to stand up to that man. He is bullying you."

"No, Carol. It's my fault. I just can't seem to make him happy anymore."

"Crap." Carol stormed out of the lounge, returning with some pamphlets on domestic abuse. "You need to read these. And I have a speaker from the domestic abuse department of the local police force coming to my class next week. You need to come."

"Oh, no. I'm not abused. It's not like that."

I didn't look at the pamphlets or go to hear the speaker, but I realized something needed to change. That night I went home and told Bob we needed to talk. He must have had some form of radar because he was instantly remorseful.

"Cathy, baby, I know I have been difficult. Business has been really stressful and I'm taking it out on you. Please be patient with me. It will be better. I promise."

I threw my arms around him, tears running down my face in relief. It would be okay now. I understood. He was just under stress.

As I began my doctoral studies, however, the tension grew. I struggled in some areas and found it more and more difficult to get the time to study and focus. Yet, I felt driven, as if I knew that my final degree would somehow be my source of freedom.

Before starting my dissertation, I had to take a series of comprehensive exams. The final exam was an oral one, and afterward I would be told I could move on. Bob was making it extremely difficult to study. In spite of everything, I passed. I was so relieved and excited. I ran home to tell Bob. He had said we would celebrate one way or another.

When I came through the door, I could tell he was drunk and angry. He had smashed some dishes and a lamp was turned over. As soon as he saw me, he began hurling insults.

"So, you are going to be a big shot now. You won't need me anymore. Well fuck you! I don't need you. You are nothing to me. Nothing. You are just a stuck-up useless bimbo. You will get your precious degree and teach in your useless school. But you will never be able to support yourself in the style you have now. Never!"

He'd never even asked if I passed. That moment was like a window had been opened and I had to escape through it. It would never get any better. Nothing I could do would be enough. Even if I quit school, he would find some other reason to hate me.

I was still carrying my bag and keys so I just turned and walked out the door. That night I stayed in the cheapest motel I could find. I couldn't even call my parents. They had been killed in a car accident a few years before. As a final gesture of anger, my father had ensured that I received nothing in their will.

After crying myself to sleep, I somehow woke with a renewed energy and hope. I called Carol, and she drove me around until I found an apartment near the school. When I knew Bob was at work, I took my clothes and a few personal belongings, leaving everything else behind. It all belonged to Bob after all, and I didn't want it. My marriage was over. But I still didn't think of myself as abused. I just felt like a failure. I had given up.

DIANA

As the group prepared to begin, a woman walked in and took an empty chair. She was tall, elegant, bi-racial, with skin like mocha and hair like burnished chocolate. Unlike the others, she held her head high, with an air of confidence as though she belonged where ever she wanted to be.

"Well, I see our new member has arrived," Janice began with a smile. "Everyone meet Diana." The group all greeted her with smiles and welcomes. Diana has joined us at the suggestion of her therapist. I will allow her to explain her circumstance to you.

Contradicting her earlier stance of confidence, Diana began to speak hesitantly. "I don't know if this is where I should be, but I am working with an attorney and a therapist through my job to try to get away from my husband before he kills me."

The group all held their breath as Diana continued. "My husband, Carl, and I were once very much in love. He joined a group of elite special forces and was deployed for two years. We had very little contact during that time, and he couldn't even let me know where he was. I have an MBA from Wharton and have a great job in a corporation—which I won't share with you. Just let me say that they are all working with me as much as possible to resolve this situation."

She took a deep breath and continued slowly. "When Carl came home, he was a different man. He had been diagnosed with PTSD and sees someone at the VA, but I don't think they are helping him. He never sleeps. He has guns stashed around the house and sometimes carries one around with him. Several times I woke to find him staring at me. Once, he asked me to open my mouth and he shoved the gun in until I began to gag. I was certain he would kill me then, but of course he didn't. The VA doesn't know that he has the guns as he is actually forbidden from owning them. I am afraid to report the guns to the authorities because it will definitely lead to a standoff and people will be killed. If they come while I am home, he will kill me first."

Diana, stood then and walked over to the coffee table and poured coffee into one of the Styrofoam cups. No one spoke.

"He says he can't live without me, and he will probably need to kill us both. He watches me constantly and calls my work incessantly to ask when I will be home. Fortunately, I am required to work long hours and I make an excellent income. He is on disability so we depend on my money. He allows me to work." She laughed at the irony of that.

I am terrified of leaving. He will find me. And when he kills me, he will likely take others with me. That is why I hesitated coming here. On Wednesday evenings he has a poker group in the basement of one of his military buddies. They play late into the night, drinking heavily and sometimes he sleeps on the couch or floor. That's why I can come here. I don't know if I want to return, but if I do, I will share my plan with you then."

For the first time since Catherine began attending the group, no one spoke, not even Janice. What was there to say. Many questions, but they all knew it wasn't the time to ask.

Janice quietly dismissed the group, and they explained to Diana how no one leaves alone as they walked her to her car, then began to drive away in twos or threes just in case someone was waiting for one of the members. It was a gloomy end to the meeting for all of them.

BOB

Bob was so drunk the night Catherine left that he barely managed to stumble into the bedroom and flop onto the bed fully clothed. When he awoke at 3 a.m., with a mouth full of dry stuffing and a desperate need to relieve himself, he noticed she wasn't in bed. Sulking, he thought. Oh, well let her sleep in the guest room again. She'll get over it. The next morning, he showered and went out searching for coffee and aspirin before heading to work. He still hadn't realized she was gone. It wasn't until that night, when he decided it was time to make up and he magnanimously brought home flowers, that he realized she wasn't there.

"Ok," he shouted as he walked in the door. "Let's get this over with. We can even go out to dinner. I forgive you. Now get in here and put these flowers in something."

There was no response, and Bob realized it was unnaturally quiet. There were no sounds anywhere in the house. Now he was getting annoyed. Finally, he stomped into the guest room. "Ok, Cathy, enough is enough."

She wasn't there; the bed hadn't been slept in. There was no sign of her. What the hell?

Grabbing a beer from the fridge, he flopped down on the sofa. Ok, she's just trying to teach me a lesson. Well, I won't bite. I can outlast her.

Two days later, Catherine still hadn't shown up. Bob called the school to be told they were on break for the next week. He checked with the bank and discovered she hadn't used their joint credit card, nor had she taken any money from the household account. What was she living on? Maybe something happened to her.

He would give it to the end of the week. If she didn't return to school, he resolved to call the police and report her missing. But then what if she was fine? People would laugh at him. Bob vacillated between fury and fear.

He started coming home early from work to see if she was back. After a few days, he realized she had been in the house. Some of her clothes were missing, and her computer. Well, the bitch better not take anything of his, he wouldn't tolerate that. But, after looking around, he realized the only things she had taken were hers. She'd even left her credit card and check book on the kitchen counter. What was she up to now?

After the week was up, Bob called the school and asked to speak to her. He was told she was in class and that they would take a message. No way. No message. At least he knew she was alive, but now the rage had overtaken the fear. How could she do this to him.

Driving to the school late in the afternoon, Bob parked at the far end of the lot where he could see the exit. He waited until he saw her come out, get into her car, and then he followed her. She pulled into the entrance to a new apartment complex just a few blocks from the school. How convenient, he thought. Then he watched as she parked in a slot and walked into the building.

Is she living with someone? Is the bitch cheating on him? Had she been planning this all along? The rage was so powerful his hands, balled into fists on the steering wheel, were shaking.

Bob started to get out of the car. He would confront her. Drag her back home. But it was a big building; he had no idea which apartment was hers. So, he waited.

He watched the entrance to the apartment until late at night, but she never came out. Slowly, he started the car and drove home. He couldn't think. After several beers, he fell into a fitful sleep, full of bad dreams. When he woke up, he knew how to get to her.

The next morning, he called his lawyer. He would divorce the bitch. He would accuse her of adultery and give her nothing. She would come crawling back to him, begging him to forgive her. Hah! He would show her.

CATHERINE

The first few months in my new apartment, I felt as though I was wandering about in a dream. Work was my escape from pain. I stayed as late as possible, finishing each detail until I faced the lonely night at home. Once the door closed behind me, I cried until sleep overtook me. There seemed to be no reason to furnish the apartment, no reason to decorate or hang pictures, or even unpack the few boxes I had brought with me. Sleeping on the floor didn't seem to matter, Until the ache in my lower back forced me to purchase a cheap blue futon. It wasn't a lot better, but a bit softer, and sleep was my other escape.

Finally, after I felt completely empty of tears, I checked my budget which permitted a tiny television set, bought at the local Kmart for $100. One more escape from the painful knot persisting in my stomach and chest. I would turn on the TV, and nibble on popcorn, which became my nightly dinner.

Due to the ten pounds I had lost over the last few months, my clothes began to hang on me. Buying new ones was not part of my frugal budget. Each night I calculated how much money I could spend on food, rent, gas and necessities. Fortunately, my car had been paid for. Since Bob always hated my small economy two-seater, there was no issue with my taking it with me.

Not only was I becoming obsessed with surviving on my meager salary, but I also began to avoid other people, with the exception of work, and of course, Carol. Carol insisted we go out to lunch at least once a week. Somehow, I felt safe with her, but still avoided discussing anything personal. It was all so painful. I knew I had failed at my marriage. What good would I ever be to anyone? I felt old, empty, and lost.

The divorce papers came to the school. Only Carol knew what they were. While she kept begging me to get my own attorney, it just didn't seem necessary. Even if I'd wanted one, I couldn't afford it anyway. I didn't want anything, there was no point in contesting his conditions. The only thing I wanted from Bob was freedom.

That was the one positive of this whole experience. When the pain in my stomach and chest began to ease, I realized that for the first time in years, I felt peace. I was free. There was no one to ask where I had been, or question what I was wearing. No one to criticize me. Most of all, I could now devote as much time as I needed to complete my dissertation. I was determined to reach my goal. I would be a Ph.D. I could use the title *Doctor*.

The library and computer lab were open until late at night and on weekends, so that students and faculty could do their research. It was exhilarating to be able to exercise my newfound freedom by spending all my time at the school, preparing my dissertation. Once I began in earnest, it seemed to take on a life of its own. It became my obsession, my life, and my future.

By the time I had to appear in court, I was nearly finished with the work that would give me that prized honor of *Doctor*. I felt fantastic. I'd even put back some of the weight I'd lost. Facing Bob was to be my final obstacle.

I walked into the courtroom alone, feeling an eerie calm. I'd expected to be nervous, but as soon as I saw him, I realized he no longer had any power over me.

Bob sat at a table across from me, flanked by two attorneys. He looked victorious. He actually smiled when the magistrate read the conditions of the divorce. I had already signed the papers, agreeing to everything. The final step was to appear to confirm in public that I did in fact agree.

When asked the question, I agreed without hesitation. At that point in time, I then glanced at Bob. The smirk that he had worn since I first saw him, slowly dropped from his face, replaced with that familiar look of anger and promised retaliation. Well, he couldn't hurt me anymore.

As we left the courtroom, Bob began shouting. "You won't get a cent from me. Ever."

Smiling, I walked toward him, placing my rings in his hand. "I don't want anything from you. Not now, not ever again."

As I walked away, I felt this euphoric feeling as though the door to hell had closed and I was now outside, and could breathe, really breathe.

Waiting in the lobby with a huge grin, was my friend Carol. I walked into her hug. I had a friend, a true friend.

"I am taking you to the best, and most fattening lunch. With wine! We laughed as we walked out of the building arm in arm. That part of my life was over. Or so I thought.

THE GROUP

Janice was preparing to open the group up for discussion when another person joined them. Diana looked slightly disheveled, but still as glamourous as she was before. Everyone turned to stare at her.

"I apologize for interrupting. Carl was late leaving for his game. I think he suspected something so I didn't leave right away. Instead, I turned on the TV and was watching the news when he burst back into the room. He looked surprised; I think he thought I was having an affair or trying to get away or something. He mumbled something about forgetting his wallet and ran back out. I still waited awhile just in case, but he never returned."

Janice shook her head. "We sometimes become just as devious as the people who are hurting us. It is a shame not to be able to trust the one person in your life who should be loyal to you, but in our case, we know we can't. It was good you trusted your instincts. What do you think triggered his reaction?"

"I probably just seemed too eager for him to leave. He has radar about that sort of thing. He even insisted we have sex right after I came home. I usually make an attempt to act as though I was enjoying it, but I guess I may have rushed it too much. Sex is the one method he has of ensuring that I am tethered to him alone. As long as he believes I want him that way, he feels safe that I won't leave him."

Rosemary muttered something to herself, and then spoke up, "I never thought it was people like you, smart, rich, beautiful people who would be hurt. Only people like me, dull, ugly, and poor. Cus, we have to take it; we got no choice, but you, you shouldn't."

Janice smiled sadly. "Abuse doesn't choose based on education, or social status, or even looks. We are all at risk."

Diana nodded. "I always felt like a strong, independent woman. It never occurred to me that this could happen to me, not me." She laughed harshly. "I loved him in the beginning, and oh yes, I loved making love with him. He was so romantic, so strong, so in control of himself. I liked that about him. I liked that he wasn't intimidated by me like many men were. But when he came back, he was different.

At first, I was very sympathetic. It was horrifying to hear even some of what he'd seen over there. What he had gone through. I went with him to his meetings. I cried with him and soothed him after the nightmares. I was certain it would get better, but then the threats started. He became obsessed about me, about not being able to live without me. He kept swearing that we would die together if I ever tried to leave him.

I knew I had to be careful, so I have been planning for over a year now. When I got my raise, I never told him. I asked them to deposit the additional money as well as my bonuses into a separate account. The rest goes into our joint account that he watches daily. That was my first step.

Next, I found a place to live that he wouldn't find. It is actually in another state. I am being transferred to a new job. I have a new phone with another number, and bought another car. The people I work with (I can't share specifics with you, just in case) are aware of my situation and they will cover for me."

"So, how are you going to get away?" Rosemary stammered.

"Well, that's the tricky part. He wants to go on a bike trip with a bunch of guys; the same guys he plays poker with. He wants me to go stay with his sister while he is gone and she agreed. What he doesn't know is that his sister is just as scared of him as I am. When he leaves my plan is to get out, fast. Then we notify the police about his guns. They will confiscate them and arrest him when he returns.

Normally, they would not confiscate guns, but since he is considered high risk, he is not allowed to keep them. For him, they are illegal. As I said before, if they came for them when he was there, it would be dangerous. He has no limits on his violence. Someone would die."

"This all sounds very risky," Janice added. "Very dangerous for you."

"I know, but my time is running out. He paces all night, shouting to himself. I think he wants to kill us both as some gesture of love or something. The bike trip is a sort of farewell to life. I believe he plans to do it when he returns. That's why I have no choice."

The group was without words. No one spoke for quite a while, not even Janice. We all knew how bad this could turn out. The group itself was even at risk if Carl discovered where she'd been going.

As they left that night, Catherine felt a coldness, an indescribable fear that she had never before experienced. It was that feeling when you know something bad is going to happen and that you have no way to stop it.

BOB

He'd parked just far enough away that he couldn't be spotted, but close enough that he would see her when she left. There were always a bunch of people coming out of the building with her. He couldn't identify them clearly, but he was certain there had to be some men mixed in. As there was no doubt the tramp was already seeing another man, or even men.

The beers he'd stashed in a cooler on the floor had hit him hard and he almost missed her tonight. Waking suddenly when he saw the lights from all the cars, he started the ignition and followed her. Not too close, but close enough so that she would always know he was there. She would learn to fear him as she never had before. The love he once had was gone. Nothing was left but hate, and the need for revenge. She'd destroyed his life; now he would destroy her.

As usual on this night of the week, she drove home and went into her apartment. And, as usual, he watched until her lights went out. But tonight, he couldn't bear to go home. He headed toward his favorite bar.

The women hanging around at this time of night were there for one thing. None of them were lookers, certainly nothing like Catherine. And none of them had her class. But he didn't want that tonight. Tonight, he wanted someone he could hurt.

Washing the blood off his hands in the dingy motel bathroom, he then threw some bills on the table beside the bed where the whore lay moaning. Closing the door behind him, Bob felt better. He'd called her Cathy the whole time he battered into her and then hitting her until she begged him to stop. Yes, it felt good. It was enough of a relief for him tonight. He could go home and sleep. He'd punished her.

He dreamed of doing the same to Catherine. He saw her face in the dream, begging and pleading with him to stop. But in the dream, he never stopped. Bob smiled in his sleep.

CATHERINE

Insight doesn't always come in a sudden flash. In my case, the awareness had been slow to arrive. The group had begun to help me to look at my relationship with Bob in a new light. I had always blamed myself, but I realized that the pain that Bob had inflicted on me was not my fault. His behavior, I now knew, was abuse.

I also was beginning to realize that, while Bob had never inflicted the physical abuse on me, it was because he was able to control me and manipulate and humiliate me. I hadn't confronted him or argued with him. It was enough for him then. Frighteningly, though, I realized that, now that he couldn't control me any longer, he could very easily become violent. I tried to shake away those thoughts, but tonight the feeling was getting stronger than ever.

As I left group, I could feel him. He was there again, I knew it. I never saw him, but I could feel him and he seemed to be getting closer. More frightening, the sense of him seemed more menacing each week.

In spite of my uneasiness about Bob, I was growing in so many ways. The group was helping me to see myself differently. I was beginning to enjoy my new status as a full-fledged doctor of literature, and an associate professor. I loved my work, and I was beginning to love my life.

I had actually made a new friend, a male friend. No, nothing romantic or sexual, but it was liberating to be able to enjoy male company, to laugh and talk without fear of retaliation or shame.

Bernie had been one of my dissertation advisors. He was in his early sixties, kind of quirky, but in a very funny way. He had snow white hair and a tiny moustache that was surprisingly dark. A highly respected intellectual, he was completely unassuming, and ingenuous.

After I defended my work, he offered to take me out to dinner to celebrate. At first, I was hesitant, but he made it very clear that it was standard and even invited a couple of the other advisors along.

Following the dinner, Bernie had called occasionally to chat. We talked about what I was teaching and he told me about his new relationship. It was casual and fun. Carol thought it was great that I had another friend. I was expanding my social circle to two, plus the group.

During one of our phone conversations, Bernie suggested that we collaborate on a paper related to my dissertation. He would enjoy taking an opposing perspective to my work. We could write it up and then present it in a debate format. We even had a venue. There was a literary conference being held in Las Vegas in October.

I was shocked that he would consider me for this, and told him I needed to think about it. The next day at lunch I told Carol and she whooped with glee.

"Of course, you will do it. And the college will pay for your expenses. You will be published. They love that. Yes, yes, yes. Tell him yes."

When I called Bernie and told him I would do it, I was still unsure. My hands shook as I made the call and I could even hear my voice quaver. He must have sensed some reservation.

"I hope you don't think this is some kind of come on, Catherine. We will have separate rooms, and we don't even have to travel together. I assure you. You have nothing to fear from me."

Carol was right, the college was thrilled that I would be published and presenting the paper at a prestigious literary conference. They quickly agreed to pay for all my expenses, and since it was over a weekend, I wouldn't need to cover my classes. My students were excited and kept teasing me about being a *star*.

As the time neared, Bernie and I met often for coffee, sometimes dinner and talked a lot on the phone. It was fun, but each time I left him I kept getting this uneasy feeling that Bob was watching and judging. What was he thinking?

BOB

He knew it. There she was with a man. Bob watched through the window of the diner as Catherine and a man laughed and ate together. He was incensed. The tramp. My God, the man was old enough to be her father. Was she that desperate?

He remembered the passion they had shared in the beginning, and he envisioned Catherine sharing that passion with this old man. It took all of his restraint not to drive his fist through the window and grab them both by the throat. But, no. There were too many in the restaurant. For now, he would find out who the man was.

It didn't take long before Bob discovered just who Bernie was. Of course, she had slept her way into that precious degree. And now they were actually planning a tryst to Vegas, of all places. Could she be any trashier? A little more digging and he knew where they would be staying. The cover, how convenient. A conference, of course.

His dreams were filled with visions of Catherine and Bernie in bed together, all twisted up in passion. Could he even get it up at his age?

The days before Catherine's trip to Vegas Bob became more and more agitated. He lived on tums and vodka, or sometimes beer—a lot of beer. His work was suffering, but he didn't care. He needed one thing, and one thing only. Revenge!

THE GROUP

There was only one topic of conversation tonight. The standoff. None of the group, not even Janice, knew if Diana had made it out of the house before the police trapped Carl in his home. It was all over the news. Carl was blockaded into his home, surrounded by police in swat gear.

They had been notified of the weapons and, thinking Carl out of town, went into the home to confiscate them based on the warrant that Diana's attorney had obtained through the AGs office. Someone must have tipped Carl off, though, because when they tried to enter the home, he began to fire on them, shooting one of the officers critically.

According to the news reports, the police were unsure if Diana was still in the home and no one had heard from her. The group knew that if she was still there, she would not likely make it out alive. The silence was a scream of fear, for Diana, and for the rest of them. They all knew it could be them.

Catherine had been so excited about her upcoming trip, and was planning to share it with them, until the news transported them in horror to that one house, and their friend Diana.

CATHERINE

I felt sick. I couldn't think of anything else. The reports showed Carl being removed from the home, seriously injured, but there was no word about Diana. Had he killed her? Was she still there, and they just hadn't reported it?

The last thing I wanted at this point in time was a trip to Vegas. I had no heart. But Carol insisted. She promised she would text me if there was any news about Diana. And I didn't feel I could let Bernie down. He had done so much for me, and his kindness had been a healing balm. I had to go.

As promised, Bernie and I were on separate flights. He had gone early to meet up with some old friends, and I chose to come the night before my presentation. Getting on the plane alone was exhilarating. I almost forgot my anxiety over Diana.

Bob and I had traveled on occasion, but it was always on his schedule and with his specific needs and purpose. I had feared talking to strangers, or had to watch what I ate or drank, or what I wore. Now I was almost giddy with the knowledge that there was no supervision, no criticism, no control. I was free. Going to a new city. I had never been to Las Vegas. Bob always said it was for degenerates and would never take me there. Although he did go himself several times to conventions with his friends.

In my window seat, I relaxed, drank a glass of wine and read a trashy novel until I fell asleep for the remainder of the flight. As we were making our descent, however, I woke with a gasp and a chill.

"Are you okay?" the young woman beside me asked.

"I'm fine. Fine."

My hands were shaking and I thought perhaps I'd had a nightmare. What was wrong with me? I'd felt so good earlier.

As we departed the plane, I focused on wheeling my carryon bag. It was as we began to enter the tram to the baggage claim and transportation area that I noticed a familiar man entering the tram through another door. It looked so much like…but it couldn't be. What would Bob be doing here?

I must be losing it, I laughed to myself. Then I began to seek out the taxi area. I was in Vegas. My euphoria returned as I breathed in the excitement of this fun city. Yes, it was overdone and quite a bit too glitzy, but I was loving it.

Checking into my room, I took a quick shower and changed into shorts and a t-shirt and set out to explore Las Vegas. I was free.

BERNIE

Bernie was kicking back in his suite with a few of his colleagues. They were reminiscing about past conferences and commiserating about books that weren't selling and jobs that were not panning out. There were some big names at the conference, but most of them were just hopeful writers and academics enjoying a week away from their students and all the pressures.

For ten years, Bernie had been happily married to his wife Laura. She was beautiful, charming, and extremely intelligent. They were both friends and colleagues as well as marital partners. They were happy. They often talked and laughed late at night, and while most long married couples dined in silence, they chatted amiably through their meals. They both thought their marriage was perfect and would last forever.

He often laughed at his male colleagues who hooked up with young grad students. How immature? He thought. What is wrong with them. Until he met Jennifer.

She was a graduate student, but had never attended one of his classes. They met for the first time at a conference, very similar to the one he was attending now. There was something different about her, something he had never felt for another woman, even Laura. He was instantly in love. He couldn't explain it to himself, or to anyone.

He kept telling himself he was such a cliché. Nevertheless, he was completely smitten. Jennifer was his soul mate; they were meant to be. The hardest part was that he would have to explain it to Laura.

Bernie told his wife the minute he returned home. He just blurted it out, filled with guilt. He cried, he was sorry, ashamed, he told her, but couldn't help himself. Bernie was completely and totally in love.

Laura was shocked, angry, and confused. What had she done wrong? Why was this happening. There has to be a mistake. But Laura knew her husband, and she knew he wasn't given to casual affairs. This was the real thing. She moved out, left the state, and filed for divorce.

Unfortunately for Bernie, Jennifer was not on the same page. They'd had a great time at the conference, she really admired him and was flattered by his attention. But she was not interested in continuing the relationship. In fact, she was engaged to a young Engineering student at MIT.

After Jennifer, Bernie had a series of relationships with younger women. He enjoyed their admiration and their energy, and of course, their soft, supple bodies. But he never fell for them the way he had for Jennifer. They were all short term and shallow.

Because of his reputation for hooking up with young graduate students, and there was a lot of speculation about Bernie's relationship with Catherine. He quickly squelched the rumors. She was his protégé, nothing else.

The attraction Bernie felt toward Catherine quickly turned to a fatherly sense of protection. Of course, she was beautiful, and her innocence was extremely appealing. He could easily have added her to his long list of graduate student conquests. However, there was a vulnerability about her that overcame his lust and instead generated his protective instincts.

Catherine's anxiety regarding her marriage and its conflicts with her career were apparent and sad. He often vacillated between fury toward her insensitive spouse and frustration toward Catherine for allowing Bob to continue dominating her. When she eventually ended the marriage, it was all Bernie could do not to break out the champagne and cheer to the entire department. Finally!

His desire for Catherine on this trip was two-fold. He wanted her to actually experience the joys and freedom that she so deserved and needed. In addition, she was his protégé and his desire to further her career was paramount in his inclusion of her into this conference. With that in mind, he organized a small gathering in one of the suites the night before their presentation. He planned to introduce her to a number of colleagues that could give her a leg up, or at least encourage her talent. Most of all, though, he desperately wanted to see her enjoy herself.

CATHERINE

I was really nervous about this party. But shopping in Vegas definitely helped. Wandering from Casino to Casino, I'd discovered some great shops, bought a new dress, something I would never have dared to wear before, and had my hair done in the hotel salon. Then, I had a long soak in the big luxurious tub. Carefully applying my make up, I fluffed up my newly coifed hair. I was ready.

Bernie met me in the lobby to escort me to the party. He was being very kind and considerate. I told him he could pick me up at the room, but he insisted that wouldn't be appropriate. Such a sweetie! I couldn't help thinking about my dad, and how I wished he could be proud of me and what I had done. I even tried calling him when I left Bob, but he refused my call, and soon after I heard they had both been killed. I was on my own. Maybe that was why Bernie's friendship meant so much.

I had no idea what to expect, but when we walked into the party, it took my breath away. I recognized so many of the faces from their book jackets, authors I had long admired. I was in awe. Bernie introduced me to every person there, but it was one man whom I never expected to meet in person who captured my full attention.

I had read every book he had written, and recognized him even before I heard his name. He looked no different from his book jacket. Perhaps a little older, maybe a little greyer, but just as handsome. He was holding court with a group of admirers when Bernie introduced me.

To my total shock, he took my hand and walked away from the group. "You, young lady, are someone I need to get to know."

I stammered my admiration for about five minutes, before he shook it off and said "enough of that nonsense. I want to hear about you."

We spoke for two hours until I began to realize that he had continued drinking steadily the entire time and was getting very drunk. He began slurring his words and getting loud. The rest of the group just ignored him, as though this was common behavior for him. He started making sexual innuendos.

At first, I was disappointed and very disillusioned. He had been my hero for so many years. A man I admired, but certainly never expected to meet. Now I just wanted to get away from him. I was starting to panic when Bernie suddenly appeared.

"I hate to break this up, but Catherine and I need to go over our notes for tomorrow."

"Oh, gosh, Bernie. You are right. I didn't realize how late it was." I began to back away from the author. "It was very nice to meet you."

Without warning, he grabbed me and aimed a wet kiss on my mouth, his tongue preparing its onslaught, but I turned as his wet mouth grazed my cheek, and waved goodbye as I walked out of the room with Bernie.

The minute the door closed behind us; we both broke into hysterics. "I am so sorry, my Dear. I was keeping an eye on you. He does get this way at parties. I know how much you've always admired him, though, and wanted you to meet him."

"Well, I don't think I will ever see him the same way again. Feet of clay, I guess."

My disappointment was outweighed by my relief that Bernie had gotten me out of there. He did escort me to my room that night, kissed me on the forehead and wished me luck the next day. We were already well prepared.

As I drifted off to sleep later the phone in my room rang several times. At first, I thought I should pick it up. It could be Bernie, or Carol. But something told me it might be the drunken author. A last final thought. Or Bob. My sleep was filled with nightmares and cold sweats.

JACK

Jack sat in the audience and watched Bernie and Catherine present their differing positions on contemporary literature. The debate was lively and fascinating. Unusual for this conference and extremely entertaining. But for Jack, the beautiful Catherine was his only focus.

Fortunately, a luncheon followed the presentation, and Jack maneuvered the seating so that he was next to her. No easy task, but definitely worth the effort. This was a woman he needed to get to know.

Catherine seemed a bit nervous when he introduced himself, but relaxed as the time wore on. They were going to the same lecture following the luncheon and he asked if he could escort her. Following the afternoon agenda, Jack requested that Catherine join him for a glass of wine in the bar. At first, she hesitated, but he promised to be a gentleman and that they would be in full view of the public at all times. He intuited her reluctance and rightly realized that she'd had a bad experience with a man, or men. He would need to take this very slowly.

As the hour passed Catherine became more open with him and shared her interests in literature. Jack told her that he was actually a professor at the same college, but in the psychology field—and he knew Carol. This latest fact eased Catherine's discomfort greatly.

Jack told her about his failed marriage—just both too young and went in different directions. She was now married with two kids and living in the suburbs. Catherine merely stated that she was divorced but avoided specifics. He could easily read her discomfort and let the subject drop.

The glass of wine became two and then led to dinner. They talked about their dreams, their work, their conflicts (not about her marriage). The entire time, though, neither noticed the man on the other side of the room glaring at them with pure hatred.

THE GROUP

Catherine entered the group filled with excitement over her trip to Vegas, but the group had more pressing issues. Diana was back.

All members were stunned to see her, as none knew how the standoff worked out. Was Diana in the house, had he killed her. They all turned toward her in expectation.

"Well, I am alive as you can see. He didn't make it though." There was a chorus of sighs in relief. Something tipped him off and he returned before the police, but I was already out of the house, and had left town. I wasn't even aware of the standoff at first, which is why I didn't call any of you.

It seems the police showed up shortly after he came home. When he saw the cars pull up, he began firing on them. They pulled back and called for reinforcements. It went on for hours until they breached the house. He took himself out before they got to him."

The silence in the room echoed each member's mix of relief for Diana, and imagining themselves in the same situation.

Janice broke the silence. "We are all grateful that Diana is safe. It is my understanding, though, that she will be leaving the state permanently and we will miss her."

"I only came tonight to fill you all in and to say goodbye. I don't know how I could have made it through all this without you. Please stay safe." At that, Diana walked out of the room with tears in her eyes, but held up her hand to indicate that no one follow her. She was gone.

"In the excitement, I haven't had the chance to introduce our newest member, Julie."

The group turned to look at the small dark-haired woman, whom none had noticed. Julie looked to be somewhere in her forties, neatly but simply dressed, and eyes that kept downcast most of the time.

"Julie," Janice asked, "Can you please tell us why you are here?"

In a quiet but determined voice, Julie began to tell her story. "I have been divorced for over ten years. My ex, Dan, comes and goes. I often wake up and he is sleeping on the sofa, or cooking in the kitchen. I tried changing the locks, but he gets the key from our youngest daughter and makes copies. I gave up. Sometimes he stays away for months."

Julie took a deep breath and continued speaking, her voice getting stronger. I began dating a man a few months ago. We are now exclusive and I was preparing to introduce him to the kids—I have three children, two girls and a boy. I have dated before, casually, but have never brought anyone home. I guess that's why Dan was never alerted or annoyed. It was for him as though nothing had changed. He could come and go as he wished.

When he discovered that I was bringing someone home to meet the children, he went into a rage. He started yelling at me, threatening to kill me. I ran to my room and tried to lock the door, but he followed me, closing the door behind us.

I saw his fist coming toward my face, and I was prepared to die. Instead of hitting me, though, he grabbed my throat, yelling over and over again that he would kill me. One of the kids started banging on the door and distracted him. I ran to the bathroom and locked myself in. I had my cell phone and dialed 911. The operator could hear him at the door, begging me to open it. She told me not to open the door until the police arrived; they were on the way."

Julie paused, breathing heavily. Janice handed her a bottle of water. After taking a few gulps, she continued. "He must have heard the sirens, because he ran out of the house before they got there. I filed a report and got a protection order. I changed the locks again and told the children to stay away from him. They had heard him threatening me, and agreed not to see him for now." She shook her head in disbelief.

I made a mistake not telling the children before about his anger. Only he usually just broke things and yelled. He'd pushed me around once, but never like this. I've done everything I can now, but I am terrified. I can't sleep, I keep gagging on anything I try to eat. I'm afraid to go to work or even to the store. They haven't arrested him yet. I don't know what else to do."

Each member of the group knew the feeling of helplessness and fear. The protection order angers them, makes them more determined to hurt. The police can only do so much.

Janice finally broke through their thoughts. "I know that the protection order is dangerous. However, it does provide a record of abuse and allows you to get help if he contacts you. If he violates the order in any way he can be arrested. If they can find him."

The last sentence hung in the air. They all knew what that meant. Unless he finds you first.

The group made a few suggestions for Julie and offered their support, but they all knew there was little they could do.

Catherine left the group that night more shaken than ever. This feeling of darkness that seemed to follow her everywhere was growing more menacing every day. Was she losing it?

CATHERINE

Driving home I couldn't stop shaking. Fiddling with the radio I found some soothing music, but that just seemed to depress me. Finally, after switching several stations, I settled on some upbeat tunes that helped a little.

Something alerted me, a flash of headlights, or the sound of an engine close behind? Was someone following me? Was that Bob's truck? The shaking returned, but with it a new feeling. Anger. Why was he doing this to me? What right did he have to torment me this way? Without some concrete evidence, I knew I couldn't report him. But I knew. It was Bob. He was following me.

I drove past my apartment building, circling until the lights behind me turned onto another street. Finally, I decided to park in front of the next building. Crossing behind the building so he couldn't see which one I entered, I came in through the back entrance. Then I ran to my apartment as fast as I could.

As I was unlocking my door, a man appeared behind me, a large bulk of a person in dark clothing. He was breathing heavily. I whirled around, my keys in my hand like a weapon, but the man, in jogging clothes, rushed past me and entered the apartment down the hall.

Gasping, I quickly opened my door, locking it behind me as I gulped back tears of fear and shame. What was I becoming? I couldn't live in constant fear the rest of my life. Tomorrow I was going to take Carol's offer of a gun. I detested the very thought of a weapon like that, but I was starting to run out of options.

The ringing phone startled me so much I dropped the glass of wine I had just poured to settle my nerves. Angrily I grabbed the phone and shouted "Damn you, Bob. Leave me alone."

I was ready to slam the phone down when Jack's voice called out, "Catherine, are you ok? Its Jack."

Sinking down on the couch with the phone cradled against me, I started to cry. "Oh, Jack, I'm so sorry. I am such a mess."

"Do you need me to come over?"

"I am so embarrassed. No, I thought you were my ex. I thought he followed me home."

"Hmm. Well, the offer is still good if you change your mind. Actually, I was calling to see if you wanted to go to dinner Saturday night. I remember you said you liked seafood and there is a new restaurant opening near the river."

My laughter was a combination of relief and excitement. A date. How about that. "Jack, I would love to, but do you mind if I meet you there?"

"I understand completely. But I would like to talk about what has you so shaken up. You don't seem like a hysterical woman. You must be in some trouble and I want to help if I can."

"I'm not sure I'm ready to talk about it just yet, but will think about it. What time? And where?"

After jotting down the particulars, I realized the shaking had abated. Cleaning up the broken glass, I then decided I needed sleep more than wine. I fell into a deep sleep almost immediately after climbing into my bed. No dreams this night. But tomorrow I was getting that gun.

BOB

He'd followed too closely this time. She spotted him. Damn! Be more careful next time. He wished he knew which apartment was hers. The buildings were locked so he couldn't check the mailboxes and didn't want to try to push himself in past another tenant. He thought she just might file a restraining order if she caught him there. He definitely needed to be more careful.

Cathy never seemed very religious, so he was surprised when he followed her to a church. It was an odd time for church services, so he guessed she had some sort of meeting there. He hadn't dared get too close, but stayed out of the lights of the parking lot. A number of cars came around the same time. He was too far away to make out who they were, but they all left together, almost like a caravan, not separating until they left the lot entirely.

What was the bitch up to now? Probably some book club or something. Was it just women or were there men there too? That's it. It was some sort of singles meet. She was meeting men there. In a church no less. What the F?

This wasn't his Cathy. She had become someone else. His Cathy would never behave that way. He hated this Cathy. He wanted to punish her. She had ruined his life. She would pay.

CAROL

Carol anticipated that Catherine would back out, but was starting to really fear that her friend might be in danger. Sure enough, when she arrived at Catherine's apartment, she was hesitant.

"Carol, I'm sorry you had to waste your time, but I don't think I can do this."

"Yeah, yeah. I hear you, but I will feel better if I know you are safe. Now, understand that the gun laws are different in every state, but since I've been through this, I can help you navigate the process. The first thing we have to do is pick out a gun."

"Don't I need to apply or fill out paperwork first?"

"Actually, you pick out the gun first, then fill out an application. Then you wait. The gun owner calls an FBI number and they run a quick background check. Once you are approved, you pay for the gun and accessories."

"Accessories?"

"Well, yeah. You will need ammo, and you probably want a safe to keep it stored when you are home. Unless you just want to put it in the drawer beside the bed."

Catherine shook her head in confusion, but went with her friend to the gun store. It was huge and filled with all sorts of people, some grim and dangerous looking, others seemed very normal and a bit nervous, as she was.

"Now there are a number of choices. I am recommending a .380 Sig Sauer rainbow. It's actually pretty."

Catherine didn't think there was anything pretty about it. It looked like a colorful, tiny, rattlesnake. "Carol, I have no idea how to use that thing."

Carol laughed. "Of course, you don't. Let's just get you the gun and then you move on to the instruction phase."

Carol gave the man behind the counter the gun and he handed her the application for Catherine to fill out. Basic stuff, enabling them to complete a background check. They wandered around until he called them back. She had been approved. Now she had to pick out ammo and decide on a safe.

The whole thing seemed like a weird dream to Catherine as she sat in the car with Carol on the way home with her new gun, ammo, and a safe that looked like a shoe box, called a gun vault.

"Okay, Cath, now you are scheduled to take classes next weekend. Then you move on to the next phase."

Catherine sighed. This was much more complicated than she'd expected. Maybe this was a mistake.

Carol felt relieved that Catherine had begun the process. Bob was becoming too much of a threat for her own comfort.

It was a surprise really. He'd seemed to love her so much, even though he was definitely possessive. Carol never thought he would go this far. When did love turn so far on its head that it became hate?

CATHERINE

The two-day training was a blur. I would never figure this out. The first day was all in a classroom. A lot of information about laws and paperwork. Cleaning and storing the weapon and safety rules. This was much more comfortable than day two.

On day two I had to practice holding and firing the gun. We shot targets that were in front of large mounds of dirt. I learned that many fatal accidents occurred when people fired at someone or something and the bullet penetrated the wall, injuring or killing the person behind it.

I was exhausted after the 16-hour weekend. Carol had driven me both days and picked me up. Probably to be sure that I didn't back out. I held the certificate of training in my hand; proof of what I had just experienced. I was numb.

"I am taking you out for dinner. First, we need to take your weapon home and lock it up."

After securing the gun and ammo in my little safe, I sank down onto the sofa.

"I don't think I have the energy to eat."

Carol pulled me to my feet. "Sure, you do. A little wine and food and you will be fine. You need to celebrate."

"Okay, but let me take a quick shower and change." I was all sweaty and grimy from the day on the range.

Carol nodded her head and proceeded to plop down to wait.

Once in the restaurant, Carol launched into the next phase. "OK, now that you have completed your instruction, you can apply for the license to carry."

I always thought it was easy to buy a gun, and I gather in some states it is easier than others. But, in this state I had to apply to the prothonotary's office, get finger printed, get affidavits from five people that I wasn't a danger to myself or others, and then wait.

The license finally arrived and it looked actually like a driver's license. But it gave me permission to carry a deadly, loaded weapon on my person at all times. Unless I traveled to another state.

At first, I felt like a hypocrite carrying a deadly weapon in my bag. I had always admonished people who touted the second amendment as an excuse for violence. But I had to admit that I felt a bit safer knowing it was there in my bag. Not that I was convinced I could actually use it. Especially on someone I'd once loved so much.

As I had the thought, I realized that the love I once had for Bob was really gone. But I didn't hate him, not the way many of the women in the group hated their husbands and boyfriends. I just didn't feel anything, except fear. I just wanted him to leave me alone so I could move on.

I hadn't told the group about the gun. I guess I was still a bit ashamed that I had betrayed my values so much. Part of me wanted to lock it up and keep it there. Or even stronger, just throw the cursed thing away. I dreaded the monthly sessions at the shooting range. Most of the people there seemed to have some kind of love affair with their weapons. Perhaps when Bob moved on, I could actually get rid of it for good. Perhaps.

THE GROUP

All eyes were on their newest member, Grace. She was much younger than most women in the group. Her blonde ponytail created a youthful look, closer to 16 than the 22 she stated in her introduction to the other members.

"My mother insisted that I join a support group in addition to my weekly counseling. But I never thought of myself as being abused. I always thought we were meant to be."

The group nodded their understanding. They had been there.

"We met when we were in high school. I was always shy and never very social. Tommy made me feel special and not so afraid. The first few months were wonderful. It wasn't until I began looking at colleges that it began to change."

More nods from the group. They could see where this was going.

"He started talking about getting married and being together forever. He said I could never survive without him. Mostly he trashed my family. They didn't understand me or love me the way he did. Then he began to belittle me; tell me no one could accept me but him.

I thought I could not ever be without him. I was nothing if he wasn't there; he was a part of me. The best part.

My parents kept pushing me to end the relationship. They were worried that it was too intense. I had no other friends. We never went anywhere, just spent all of our time together.

He started threatening to kill himself if I ever left him. He started doing drugs and getting into scraps with other guys he thought were hitting on me. I finally decided to end it. I couldn't breathe, and I started having panic attacks.

Tommy called day and night. He followed me home from school and sat outside my house in his car. Eventually, my parents filed a complaint with the police, and he stopped showing up. He'd graduated the year before and wasn't in school anymore."

Grace took a deep breath and Janice handed her a bottle of water. After several gulps, she continued.

"I got accepted into my first choice of colleges and left a few months later. At first it was hard to concentrate, but I actually began to relax and even made friends. And I met a guy, a great guy. We recently got engaged."

The group eagerly congratulated her, but began to wonder why she was there.

"The problem is that Tommy actually took his own life after my engagement. I feel I haven't talked to my fiancé about my feelings. Mostly, though, I don't know who I am without Tommy. My therapist said it is because I never developed my own identity while I was with him. My existence was always whatever he needed from me. I never went through that independent teenage stage when I rebelled and wanted to *find* myself. I need to discover who I actually am and what I really want out of life so I can grow as a person. I can't get married until I do that."

Grace looked up, tears in her eyes. "So that's why I'm here."

For one of the few times, the group was actually silent. Janice quietly spoke, "That's what these abusers do, they destroy you, leaving nothing of who you really are or were. We often confuse the emotional dependence with love and find it difficult to separate from them. In Grace's case, he never let her find out who he was."

As they all left for the night, each member hugged Grace and let her know she was welcome.

She was smiling when she left.

CATHERINE

My entire closet was piled on top of the bed. What should I wear? Casual? Dressy? Sexy? Oh, no not that. I had no idea. I hadn't been on an actual date since before Bob. Why was I so nervous? This wasn't a serious relationship. It was just dinner. I finally settled on a pair of casual slacks and a sweater I had to dig from the bottom of a pile. Not too wrinkled. Just tossed them into the dryer for a few minutes. They looked okay, but not too fancy. Didn't want to send the wrong impression. Nevertheless. I was excited.

Walking into the restaurant my nerves returned in full force. What am I doing? This is crazy. I started to turn around and run out of the restaurant when I spotted Jack. He stood from the table, smiling, and waved me on. I couldn't leave now.

There was something about Jack that always calmed my nerves. He was easy where Bob was intense, gentle and accepting, where Bob was hard and demanding. He could laugh at himself and wasn't defensive. So relaxing. I had always been on edge with Bob, terrified of saying or doing the wrong thing. I had no such fears with Jack.

He immediately launched into an amusing story of his last student conference where the young woman actually thought he would change her grade if her skirts were short enough. We both laughed at the presumption of the young. Then he ordered wine, and the meal progressed in laughter and fun until he asked the question.

"What had you so frightened on the phone the other night?"

I had no intention of discussing this with Jack but he seemed so warm and interested, and I loved the way his blue eyes sparkled and the lines around them crinkled when he smiled. He made me feel safe and trusting, so unlike Bob, who always seemed ready to explode.

I didn't realize how much I needed a comforting backboard to bounce off my thoughts. At first, I was hesitant and a bit fearful, but he didn't comment, just listened and murmured sympathetically from time to time. Toward the end, though, Jack began to look alarmed.

"Cat. Oh, gosh is it okay if I call you Cat? It just seems to suit you."

I merely nodded. No one had ever called me Cat. It was like a new identity. I liked it.

"Cat, this man sounds dangerous. I am starting to worry about your safety."

"Well, I confess I did get a gun."

"Wow. That doesn't sound like you." Jack sat back in his chair.

"No, it isn't. I'm actually having a hard time with the idea. But Carol convinced me I needed protection."

Jack didn't comment for a few minutes, then turned very serious. "You might want to contact the police, and file a protection order."

"That's the problem. He hasn't actually done anything. I can't prove the calls are from him and I just have this premonition that he's always there. I get this chill, but never really see him."

He reached across the table then and touched my hand. The touch was very warm and gentle, but I jumped, knocking over my water glass. I could feel the tears in my eyes, as I stammered my apology.

"It's only water, Cat. Look, the glass was nearly empty anyway. No harm done."

"I think I was reacting to the touch. No man has touched me since Bob. If anyone came even close to me, he would glower, warning them off, then he would blame me and say I was egging them on.

Once, a neighbor hugged me after the funeral of a classmate who was killed in an accident. It was a friendly, supportive gesture, but I thought Bob would hit him. He punished me for days afterward."

"Punished you? Did he hit you?"

"No, No. It was never like that, more like emotional torture." I shook my head, unable to explain further.

"Look, I know we came in separate cars, but I am following you home. I will walk you to your door, and I promise I won't ask to come in, but I need to know you got home safely. I also want to check your locks, and I think you need a security system."

I didn't argue, but allowed Jack to follow me out of the restaurant. Then I felt the familiar chill. I only saw his back, but I somehow knew it was Bob. He had been there watching me the whole time. I felt like I was going to lose the lovely dinner I had just eaten. Will it never end?

THE GROUP

At first no one noticed the new member. She was sitting so silently in the back of the room, her head down. It almost appeared that she was asleep. Then Janice motioned for her to take a seat in the circle.

"Carlyle why don't you introduce yourself."

Without speaking, the woman stood and began taking off her jacket. The group could immediately tell this was no ordinary woman. Her clothes, while very understated were definitely of designer quality.

She delicately placed her jacket on the back of her chair and began to unbutton her blouse. The group was mesmerized. It was then that they saw the deep myriad of colorful bruises lining her chest and stomach. She quickly rebuttoned the blouse and took a seat.

Her face was streaked with the tears of humiliation and shame that they had all experienced. "My name is Carlyle, but I would love it if you would call me Carly. Julian and my parents refused to allow anyone to use the nickname I loved, but they won't know in here."

In spite of her apparent shame, Carly held her head with dignity and strength. This was a woman with determination and courage.

"I had always been told that abused women were all from trailer parks, never upper-class neighborhoods. I've learned that nothing is further from the truth. And some might think it is easier to get out when there are financial resources. Also, not always the truth. I showed you the bruises beneath my blouse because Julian never blemished my face. Not a good look for his wife at the charity events.

The long sleeves and high neck covered any evidence of his recent wrath.

My wedding was the social event of the year. My mother was in ecstasy. My father was proud. Even though he'd never had the son who would continue the family name, his daughter had made a good match. Julian was a catch.

It wasn't until I gave birth to his daughter, rather than the son he'd expected that Julian began the abuse. Prior to that, even though he was cold and detached, he was always polite and respectful. After Cindy was born, he left on a business trip. He never called or contacted me during his absence. When he returned, I was walking down the stairs, holding our daughter. The servants were away for the day, and I had planned to take her for a walk in the garden.

Julian took one look at me, grabbed my arm and flung the baby and me down the stairs. Then he walked out the door. The servants found me when they returned and called an ambulance. I told them I fell. Cindy didn't survive. He never touched me again sexually, but began nightly beatings before bed, calling me names and telling me what a disappointment I was."

Carly took a breath, but the group stayed silent and waited for her to continue.

"I went to my mother, begging her to let me come back home, but she kept asking what I had done to anger him. She told me to never mention this to my father and to go right home and fix things with my husband.

He doesn't really care what I do as long as I attend the proper functions and appear beside him when necessary. I found a brochure about domestic abuse in the church and that's how I came here."

When it became clear that Carly had finished sharing, the group all moved toward her and gently took her into a group hug.

Janice motioned them to retake their seats and began to speak. "Sometimes it becomes harder to get out of an abusive situation when you are in a high-profile environment. I realize that your family isn't going to be any help to you, but what about friends?"

"Oh, I have a lot of friends. We go to luncheons and work on charity events. But they would never understand the abuse, and if I left, I would lose everything. I would never hear from them again."

"They don't really sound like friends."

Carly laughed. "Well, their friendship is based on my social status. If I left, I would no longer be of any value to them, just an embarrassment or a reminder of what could happen to them. I signed a prenup, and would have nothing. I would be lucky if I escaped with the clothes on my back. He would trash my reputation. I would definitely be on my own."

"Well," one of the group interrupted, "you were able to get a good education. You could probably get a decent job."

"My education taught me how to use my social status. I took languages, art and music appreciation, nothing that would make me employable. I was never expected to work. If I left, I would have nothing. I have no idea where I would go or how I would live."

Some of the group still looked confused. How could someone of her status ever be broke and alone? Even Catherine, who left with nothing had managed to support herself, but then she'd already had a job.

Only Janice nodded in understanding. "Carly, if you will remain after the others leave, I will go over some options with you."

Carly nodded her assent and the rest of us moved toward the exit for the night.

BOB

He watched her enter the restaurant alone. Maybe she was meeting a friend, but then he spotted the man. Sliding into a seat at the bar he watched as they laughed together. At one point, the man took her hand, his hand, the hand that belonged to him, no one else. How dare he touch her! She was his.

He had several beers. No stomach for food. He was filled with such rage. He visualized ripping the man's face and then choking Cathy until she could no longer breathe. How could she do this to him?

Then he saw them begin to leave the table. Throwing money down on the bar, he quickly walked out to his car before she could see him.

When Bob reached his car, he threw up violently before he opened the door. Probably not good to drink so much on an empty stomach, but he was too furious to eat. He watched as she got in her car alone. Well, that was good. But then he realized the man was following her out of the parking lot.

Following closely behind, he saw them both park and walk inside together. The slut! She was going to sleep with him. She would let him touch her in places that belonged only to him. How could she do this? But soon, the man returned to his car and drove off. Hah! She'd rejected him. Good for her. But he couldn't let this happen again. Never again. He needed to stop her.

THE GROUP

As the group began to filter in, they gasped in surprise at the familiar face. Diana was back. What was she doing here? Her abuser was dead and she had moved on. What was going on.

Janice began the meeting by addressing their surprise. "As you can all see, Diana has returned to us. Before you bombard her with questions, Let's allow her to explain."

Diana began to talk. She seemed to have lost the cool confidence they'd seen before. This was a new shaken Diana. "When I left here, I thought it was all over. He'd been killed in the standoff with the police. I was free. I moved on. Or so I thought."

She took a long drink of water and continued. "I had to come back to settle the house, and I needed to get my things out of it. Things I'd forgotten. But when I went there, I couldn't go in. I began to shake and turned and ran. I am staying in a hotel for now, but I realized it isn't over. I dream about him almost every night. I see him in places that I know he couldn't possibly be."

Diana began to sob. "I can't get rid of him. He's always there."

Grace, who was usually very quiet and subdued chimed in. "I feel the same. He died, I know he died, but I hear his voice at night. Sometimes I hear him call my name. It sounds like he's in the walls."

The others nodded their understanding, and Catherine felt a shock of agreement. It wasn't over for her either. It wouldn't be over unless she did something to stop him. But what? How?

CARLY

Carly listened to the options Janice laid out for her; none seemed viable. She drove home in a daze. Hearing the words of Janice and the others, she realized that the so-called friends and social status were meaningless. She had no life of her own. She looked around at the beautiful house, filled with expensive furniture. The gleaming dining room table would easily seat over 20 for a sit-down dinner. The staff came in daily to clean and polish, but Julian refused to have anyone live-in. He needed the privacy for his nightly beatings. She shuddered.

But tonight, Julian was away. She never knew for sure exactly where he went, but he didn't seem worried about her leaving. He had made sure that she was trapped by her life-style. She could never leave him. She'd be a fool.

Entering her bedroom, Carly opened her closet and gazed at the racks of expensive clothing, some with tags still attached. Beneath the racks were rows and rows of shoes, for dress, for casual, even for yoga. All with designer labels.

She shook her head and went to a box at the top of her closet. She took out a pair of jeans, sneakers, and a sweatshirt that she had purchased from target on a whim. They'd never been appropriate for anything, but she put them on now. Taking off her rings and jewelry, she carefully put them in the box on top of her bureau. Satisfied that she no longer wore anything of value, she reached far back in the closet to a shoe box containing beautiful, unworn leather boots. Inside the boots was a few hundred dollars in cash she had managed to save over the years. Just a few dollars at a time, enough so that Julian would never notice.

Putting the cash in her sweatshirt pocket, she left her purse, her phone, and credit cards in the top drawer. She didn't want him to notice her absence immediately when he returned. He would just think she was out.

Carly then drove to a mall nearby. Leaving the car, with the keys in the cup holder, she walked to the bus stop at the edge of the mall. She had taken this bus numerous times, but always kept her car keys and returned in a few hours. This time she would not come back.

There was a motel at the end of the bus route that rented by the week. A diner next to the motel advertised needed help. Carly had no idea if she could wait tables, but doubted they would be too picky and hoped she would learn fast.

Carly was now very alone, and with very little money, but she was free. For the first time in years, she smiled.

JACK

He couldn't stop thinking about her. He'd always enjoyed the company of women, but when they were out of sight, they were proverbially out of mind. Not so with Catherine. He kept seeing her face, the fragility, and yes, the fear. How could he help her?

He'd called last night after she came home from her group and could tell she was clearly shaken. "I have your new locks, and the alarm system should be installed tomorrow. I know its late, but is it okay if I come over and put in the locks. I hate to wait any longer. The one you have is useless."

Catherine laughed. "Of course, come ahead. I just bought a bottle of wine. You can help me drink it."

Jack arrived shortly with a second bottle of wine. "To replace the one we drink tonight."

He could tell she was upset, but didn't comment right away. "Let me get this lock in so I feel better. Hard to sleep at night thinking of you alone."

Catherine looked touched by his concern. "Well, I do have a gun."

Jack jumped slightly. "I respect your need to protect yourself, but I really do hate those things."

"Actually, I do too, but it is locked in its safe for now. Not to worry. Funny, though, the more I practice with it, the more comfortable I am with it." She shook her head, "not that I agree with guns in general, but it does provide a sense of security. I doubt, though, when it comes down to it, I could actually shoot someone. I don't know. Maybe?"

Jack chuckled. She was so adorable. "Let's have that wine now."

They sat comfortably, sipping their wine, talking about their classes, politics, life in general. They both had the same basic beliefs, which was such a relief for both of them. It was always so stressful to be out with someone that chose to argue over what seemed like obvious common rights. It was as though some people felt threatened by power that wasn't under their control.

The more he was with her, the more Jack felt drawn to Catherine. When he stood to leave, he felt unable to stop himself from gently pulling her toward him and touching her lips to his. This time his touch seemed welcoming as she leaned in toward him and returned his kiss.

He opened the door to leave, took one look at her, her lips flushed with the kiss and those eyes melting into his. Without hesitation, he closed the door behind him and drew her into a deeper and more passionate kiss. Before they knew it, they were on the sofa, their hands exploring each other fearlessly.

Catherine always seemed so shy, Jack was amazed at her passion and response. He wanted more, and it took all his strength to finally pull away. "Cat, oh Cat, I want you so much, but I don't want to rush you. Please think about me, and let me call you tomorrow. Ok?"

Catherine smiled, smoothing down her clothes and catching her breath. "Wow, I never thought I could feel that way again. I'm kind of embarrassed. I hope I didn't shock you."

"You are so adorable! I'll call you tomorrow. Sleep well, and lock up behind me."

Jack saw her face, and felt the touch of her smooth, milky white skin, all night long. In the morning he watched the time until he felt it was ok to call her. Just hearing her voice warmed his heart. Is this what it's like to fall in love?

THE GROUP

Janice began the session with a question. "How many of you have children"

Mazy, Susan, and Rosemary raised their hands.

"How do you feel your abuse has affected your children? We should have talked about this sooner, but I feel we need to discuss it now. All three of you are still with your spouses."

Rosemary, who seldom spoke, began speaking immediately. "I think," she began "that it is harder to leave when you have children. Nobody wants to take in a battered wife, let alone three kids. The shelters are crowded. Plus, the biggest reason, is if he kills me, what happens to them? My oldest boy is starting to mimic his father. He hits his sisters and gets in fights at school. When I try talking to him, he yells and lately actually threatens me.

I admit that I still love my husband, but is it fair to the kids to stay and damage them in that way? I never really thought about how it affected them emotionally. I always just thought if they were physically safe, they would be okay." She started to cry silently and repeated, "What have I done? What have I done?"

The others were nodding. Susan jumped in. "Well, I finally did leave, but it wasn't easy. You are right. None of my family wanted to take on my mess. But he'd started hitting my youngest and that did it for me. When I tried to stop it, that's when he broke my wrist. That gave me enough to get the police to take him away long enough to move into a shelter. And I found a job.

It was like a miracle. I had no clothes. The only shoes I had were flip flops and I had bruises all over my face and arms, but this man who owns a small business, hired me on the spot. I will never forget the look he gave me when I walked in the door. I was terrified that he would throw me out. I looked frightening. I started to stammer, to explain and apologize for my appearance, but he gently helped me into a chair and brought me coffee. We talked for over an hour. He went into his safe and handed me some money, told me to take the money, get some food and clothes and be back ready to work on Monday.

I later learned that his sister had been the victim of abuse and he recognized the bruises and the fear immediately. Later, when he learned I was living in a shelter, he advanced me enough to rent a small house. I'm learning to do the books, and I'm going back to school. I thank God every day for him.

But, no, it isn't over. I am afraid every day. And my kids? My kids wake up screaming at night. They refuse to ride the bus for fear he will find them. They avoid all social activities. They come home and hide in their rooms. The youngest still wets the bed."

Janice shook her head. "Yes, we should have talked about this sooner. We know what we are going through, our fears, and our anxieties. But our children are often faced with a trauma that stays with them for life.

Mazy rubbed the scar down her neck. "I never talked about this before. The night I got this," she pointed to the scar," he tried to kill me. I fought him. Hard. He had a knife. My son tried to help me. He was only ten, but he was so brave. He grabbed for the knife and they struggled. I jumped in and he slashed me. I passed out. When I woke up. They were both gone. My beautiful boy and his evil father. Both covered in blood." Mazy began to sob as the group tried to comfort her, but she motioned them away. "No. wait. I need to say more. My daughter was only four. She was in her room and slept through it all. But she misses her father. As evil as he was to us all, she misses him. I think she blames me that he is gone."

Mazy looked back up with eyes that revealed her empty grief.

Janice jumped in. "It is often surprising that children want the very people that have abused them, or have abused someone they loved. But it is human nature to want to be loved, even when it makes no sense.

This is why we have initiated a series of small groups for children in varying age groups. We want to show children what a normal family should look like, and how to protect themselves both physically and emotionally. Many children who grow up in dysfunctional homes accept the abhorrent behavior as normal. They then proceed to perpetuate the very behavior they feared. Our goal is to stop that process, to show them how they can access support and help and how they can break out of that tragic cycle."

The group all nodded, many in shame for allowing their children to suffer. Rosemary shook her head in shock. "I always thought I could hide it from them and that they would be ok, but I realized the only secret was the one I kept from myself."

The group dispersed to sign their children up for the appropriate groups and discuss how to proceed further. Mazy would need individual counseling for her daughter as well as group. It would be a long journey for all of them, and never completely forgotten.

JACK

Jack waited for Catherine outside group to drive her home. She told him it was totally unnecessary, but he had been increasingly worried lately. The calls had increased, and she often felt like she was being followed.

Tonight, though, he only went inside long enough to ensure that it was safe for her. Kissing her gently on the lips, he left, promising to call the next day.

He waited until he heard the locks click, then walked out to his car, looking around for any strange vehicles. He didn't notice the dark pickup just around the corner.

Driving home, Jack realized just how much he had come to care for Catherine and how desperately he was worried about her. He believed that Bob was dangerous, but until he actually did anything overtly, the police had no grounds to arrest him. They put a tracker on her phone, but the calls were very brief, just long enough to distress her. And Jack.

Jack was so deep in thought that he didn't notice the headlights behind him until the glare made him shade his eyes. "What the???"

He tried to wave the vehicle past, it looked to be a pickup but the glare was so overwhelming that he couldn't really tell for sure. Speeding up, slowing down, nothing seemed to make a difference. The truck didn't pass him, nor did it hit him or attempt to run him off the road. It just stayed directly behind him until he reached his driveway.

Jack hit the garage door opener, drove into the garage, and closed it behind him. The truck never tried to follow him into the drive but sped away. All too fast to get a license number or even a description. The problem was, though, that the driver now knew where he lived.

Throughout the night Jack wrestled with what to do with the incident. He called the police in the morning and they said that the worst they could get the driver on was aggressive driving, but even then, they had no idea how to find him. They couldn't go on speculation. And they had nothing on Bob.

Jack waited until late that morning before calling Catherine.

"Cat, honey, there's something I need to talk to you about. Is it ok if I stop over tonight?"

"Sure. Why don't you come for dinner? I have to warn you, though, it will be very simple. I am no Martha Stewart."

"Thank God! I prefer simple. I will bring wine."

"Perfect, see you at 7."

CATHERINE

My first dinner party in my very own apartment. Ok, so only dinner for two, but it was mine. I get to pick the food, cook it, and set the table without worry. The chicken was marinating in the kitchen, salad waiting for dressing, and I just put a mason jar full of wild flowers on the center of my tiny table when Jack arrived.

Over the past few months, as my depression began to lift, I began to view my tiny apartment as my personal haven. I bought paint and spent evenings and weekends brightening up the rooms with splashes of color. Inexpensive throw pillows added to its personality. I even bought some colorful dishes and glasses I'd discovered at an outdoor flea market. Framing some of the book jackets from my favorite books gave the walls an important touch of home, of me. It was far from the luxury Bob had created, but it was mine, and I loved it.

I wasn't sure when I'd begun to get a rush at seeing Jack, but it had become almost expected when I opened the door. He was looking so handsome and sweet, holding a bottle of wine in one hand and a bouquet of, oh yes, wild flowers in the other. He laughed when he saw the ones on the table. "Great minds?"

"Definitely." Taking them from him I found a matching mason jar and positioned them on the coffee table, where the wine glasses waited.

"As I said, I am not a gourmet cook. Bob prided himself on his grill. He bought this enormous grill and took charge of most of our meals. I was basically his sous chef, bringing him the things he demanded. I seldom attempted a meal without his instructions, so I stopped trying. We are having pan grilled chicken thighs (I know breasts are healthier, but I prefer the thighs), salad and olive bread with real butter. Nothing fancy."

"That sounds wonderful. I actually dated a few women over the years who were declared gourmets. They always cooked chicken breast and no matter what fancy sauces they cooked them in I always found them dry and tasteless. The meals took forever, looked beautiful, but not to be enjoyed,"

"Well, here's to simple, and tasteful. No grill in this apartment, but I find that this pan will do the job. Let me just put them on to simmer while I open this beautiful bottle of wine."

Time just seemed to flow with Jack. We chatted through dinner. I made coffee and brought out the special dessert. "OK, here's to simple."

"Wow, ice cream bars. My favorite. How did you know?"

"Well, I didn't but I figured it was one thing I couldn't mess up. I actually tried baking a cake and it looked like we had been hit by an earthquake while it was in the oven. The birds are enjoying it now."

Jack's laughter was contagious until I looked into his eyes and saw that there was something serious he was holding back.

"Cat, honey, I didn't want to tell you this over the phone, but something happened last night". Jack went over the incident with the truck in as much detail as possible. "There was nothing I could use to report it. He didn't actually hit me, or attempt to run me off the road. It was just like he was taunting me. I thought you should know. Cat, I really don't think you should drive alone at night."

"Jack, you can't be with me every minute. And I wouldn't want you to. I was a virtual prisoner for years. I won't let him do this to me anymore. And I can't allow you to do it either, even if you mean well,"

"I understand, I just want you to be careful." He took my hands. "I couldn't stand it if anything happened to you."

"Jack, I need to think about this. I'll call you tomorrow."

"Ok. I understand. I… I'll talk to you later."

My mind was racing three miles ahead. I opened the door, kissed Jack tenderly but briefly and closed the door firmly behind him. Without bothering with the door locks, I picked up the phone. "Bob, I need to see you. I'm coming over." I didn't wait for a response, just grabbed my lethal friend out of his protective home, put it securely in my bag, and walked out the door.

BOB

Catherine's coming home. She'll be here soon. What could she want? Of course, she wants to come back to me. She realizes what a fool she's been. He'd dreamed of this for months now. She'd beg him on her knees to take her back. Oh, what joy!

Of course, he'd take her back, but she'd have to work for it. He wouldn't be easy. And, of course, she'd need to be punished to learn her lesson.

Bob looked around him. The place was a mess. No time to clean up. But it was her fault. She could clean it up. Part of her punishment. He needed a shave, No time for that either. She could have given him more notice.

The doorbell rang. She was here. At last. His pain would be over soon. Her pain was just beginning. He smiled as he went to the door.

CATHERINE

I thought I would be shaking with fear and anxiety, but surprisingly I felt an eerie calmness. It would be over soon. One way or another.

Ringing the bell, only once, I knew he heard it, just as I knew he was taking his time. One of his ways of punishing me. It was almost funny. But then, I had lost my sense of humor on the drive over.

The door opened and Bob sauntered away. As he turned to look at me, I realized he believed I was back for him, to beg his forgiveness. I almost laughed then.

Shaking my head in amazement I finally found my voice. "Jack, this isn't what you think. I'm not back. I will never be back."

The look of shock and growing fury changed his face from smug to snarly bright red.

"You bitch. You've ruined my life. I hate you, hate you."

When I didn't answer, he continued in a growl. "So, I guess now you hate me. Me. After all I did for you."

"No, Bob. I really don't hate you. I suppose I should after what you put me through, but I don't hate you. Actually, I don't feel anything for you now." The words shocked me as I realized how true they were. My only feeling for him was total apathy.

"I'm here today because this craziness has to stop. You can't keep terrorizing me and my friends. If you keep this up, I will have you arrested. I mean it, Bob. It's over. Walk away. Get your life back."

I waited and watched silently as I could see the realization hit him. The rage grew. It was coming, I could see it, and I was ready. My hand went into my pocket and circled the gun. This was it.

In one snarl he was at me. His hands circled my neck and he kept screaming, "You bitch, you bitch, I will kill you."

I could feel my breathing getting more and more pressured, and I knew the world was going to go black in a minute until I felt the pressure lessen and saw him step back. He had my gun in his hand. When did he take it from me? I didn't even feel it leaving my fingers.

"So, you came here to kill me? Well, surprise, I have the gun now."

He kept waving the weapon in front of me. I stood silent, not moving, trying to get my breathing back.

"I could shoot you right now. The gun is yours. You came here to kill me. We struggled for the gun. It was self-defense." Bob started pacing back and forth, rambling on and one until he turned and aimed. "I hate you. You deserve to die."

I watched with awe as his face changed, his eyes widened in surprise.

"Oh, God what am I doing? I love you, Cathy. I've always loved you." In a sudden move he turned the gun on himself, put it to his head and pulled the trigger.

The silence was deafening. There was only a tiny click.

I reached over and took the weapon out of his limp hand. "Did you really think I would bring a loaded gun in here? Did you not know me at all?" I turned toward the door, shaking my head. As I closed the door behind me, I dialed 911. "I want to report an attempted suicide."

EPILOGUE

This was my last meeting with the group. Bob had spent the last two months in a mental health facility getting much needed help. His doctors say he has a long way to go, but I no longer fear him. No, I don't hate him. Not yet ready to feel sorry for him, but my feelings are pretty neutral right now, which is best for me.

"I just want to say goodbye to all of you, and thank you for everything. You opened my eyes and made me see that abuse is not always obvious. It is not always physical, but it is always destructive. Most importantly, it is never your fault. You are all courageous, strong women. You cope in different ways, but you cope. You keep going, keep living. I love you all!"

Carly, now dressed in her now familiar attire of jeans and sweatshirt, smiled broadly. "You should all know that I have gone back to school. It seems that our lovely State provides free community college to lower income people. Go figure. I'm taking classes in bookkeeping and some other useful skills. I've even started looking for another job, although I admit I've become a pretty good server in the diner. And the customers appear to really like me. I have a uniform, so I don't need to buy more clothes.

The biggest surprise is that Julian found me and was thrilled to give me a quiet divorce as long as I didn't ask for anything. My parents have completely disowned me, and forget my "friends," but life is pretty good right now."

The group actually applauded. Good news was pretty rare.

"I don't want to upstage you," Grace interceded, "but I have some good news as well. I talked to Kurt, my fiancé. It was a very long and painful conversation, but we agreed to put off the marriage or even a discussion of marriage until I had worked out my issues over Tommy. Therapy is going well, and happily I do have the support of my family."

It was so rewarding to hear of the success of some of the group. Although others were still struggling. Rosemary had not yet been able to break with her abuser, but her children were in therapy as was Mazy's daughter. Hopefully they will make it out.

Diane had come back to the group from time to time and was feeling more confidant and secure each day. She admits that she has no idea when she will trust enough to enter another relationship, but is satisfied to just work on herself and her career for now.

There were tears and many hugs as well as some thoughtful gifts and drawings from these brave women who had saved my life. When I walked away, I was at peace.

Jack leaned against his car smiling as he saw me. My new life was just starting.

www.ingramcontent.com/pod-product-compliance
Lightning Source LLC
LaVergne TN
LVHW011733060526
838200LV00051B/3164